GARTH WILLIAMS

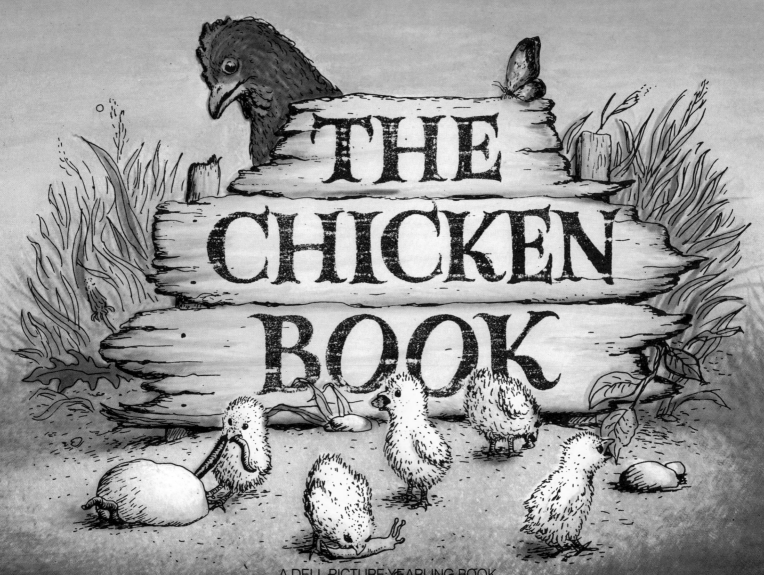

THE CHICKEN BOOK

A DELL PICTURE YEARLING BOOK

Published by
Dell Publishing
a division of
Bantam Doubleday Dell Publishing Group, Inc.
666 Fifth Avenue
New York, New York 10103

For information address Delacorte Press, New York, New York 10103.
The trademark Yearling® is registered in the U.S. Patent and Trademark Office.
The trademark Dell® is registered in the U.S. Patent and Trademark Office.
ISBN: 0-440-40600-5
Reprinted by arrangement with Delacorte Press
Printed in the United States of America
April 1992

10 9 8 7 6 5 4 3 2 1
LBM

The Chicken Book

Said the first little chicken,

With a queer little squirm,

"I wish I could find

A fat little worm."

Said the next little chicken,

With an odd little shrug,

"I wish I could find

A fat little slug."

Said the third little chicken,

With a sharp little squeal,

"I wish I could find

Some nice yellow meal."

Said the fourth little chicken,

With a small sigh of grief,

"I wish I could find

A little green leaf."

Said the fifth little chicken,

With a faint little moan,

"I wish I could find

A wee gravel stone."

"Now, see here," said the mother,

From the green garden patch,

"If you want

any breakfast,

Just come here

and